410

O9-ABI-257

HOLIDAY COLLECTION

The Princess and the Kiss

The Three Gifts
of Christmas

By Jennie Bishop

Illustrations by Preston McDaniels

Library of Congress Cataloging-in-Publication Data

Bishop, Jennie.
  The princess and the kiss : the three gifts of Christmas / by Jennie
Bishop ; illustrations by Preston McDaniels.
    p. cm.
  Summary: A good king and queen, hoping to teach their ungrateful daughter
the true meaning of Christmas, decree that no one is to bring presents to
the royal family and, instead, they give the princess only three gifts, each
as precious as she, herself.
  ISBN 978-1-59317-378-4 (casebound)
  [1. Conduct of life–Fiction. 2. Gifts–Fiction. 3. Princesses–Fiction. 4.
Kings, queens, rulers, etc.–Fiction. 5. Christmas–Fiction.] I. McDaniels,
Preston, ill. II. Title.

PZ7.B52725Pri 2009
[E]–dc22

2009011992

Text ©2009 by Jennie Bishop

Illustrations ©2009 by Warner Press

ISBN: 978-1-59317-378-4

Published by Warner Press, Inc, 1201 E. 5th Street, Anderson, IN 46012

Design Layout: Kevin Spear   Editors: Robin Fogle, Karen Rhodes

Printed in Singapore

Warner
Press Kids™
educate • nurture • inspire
www.warnerpress.org

nce upon a time a king and queen were known far and wide for the purity and peace they brought to their kingdom. The queen, as a princess, had kept her kiss for a man of honor. This good man, who had saved his kiss as well, became ruler of the kingdom by proving his courage and pure heart.

This happy couple had a daughter of their very own whom they loved dearly. As part of the royal family, she enjoyed all the privileges of being wealthy—especially at Christmastime. Visitors filled the castle for an entire month of celebration and of course everyone brought presents for the charming little princess, who usually expressed her thanks with warm hugs and an open heart.

Sadly, the princess grew to be ungrateful. Her parents watched with disappointment as she tore into Christmas gifts without thought. She tossed many beautiful toys aside with a muttered "Thank you," and the question, "What else is there?" The king and queen, who had taken special care to raise their daughter with manners suited to a royal family, were heartsick and distressed. And so they arrived at a plan to cure the princess of her selfishness, a plan that began weeks before Christmas with an important announcement.

"Do you remember the Christmas story, dear?" the queen asked.

The girl nodded. "Oh yes, Mother. I remember the story of the Baby and the angels and that wicked King Herod."

"I'm glad you brought up old King Herod," said her father. "He was a selfish man, wasn't he? What made him so selfish?"

"He wanted to kill the Baby to keep his throne," said the girl, bowing her head.

"Yes," answered her mother. "And what made the three wise men different?"

"They brought gifts instead," said the little girl, "which is why we receive gifts at Christmastime."

"That's right," said the king. "The wise men brought three gifts."

The king and queen looked at each other. "Darling," began her mother, "would you like to become a part of the Christmas story this year? We will give three gifts as well, just like the wise men."

The girl's eyes lit up. "Really, Mother? To who?"

"To whom," corrected her father. "And the three gifts will be for you, my dear."

Now the look on the princess' face was one of horrified surprise. "Only... three?" she squeaked. In her mind danced memories of chocolates, beautiful birds in cages, a horse of her own, and whole collections of china figures brought from the eastern countries. How could Christmas be the same with only three gifts? A tear of disappointment ran down the princess' cheek.

Her parents came close and wrapped her in their arms. "We will also give up our gifts this year, precious girl," said her father gently. "And our gifts to you will be given on the first day of Christmas instead of the twelfth, as has been the custom. Then you will be able to enjoy them for all twelve days of the holiday."

"Do you understand, my dear?" asked the queen. The princess nodded, but she felt very sad indeed.

hristmas parties welcoming the holiday that year seemed strange to everyone. The citizens of the kingdom, by royal decree, brought no gifts to the royal family. Although feasting, fun and games still took place no presents arrived for the family in the castle.

Every time the princess thought of presents she felt her stomach tighten into a knot.

"Only three presents," she reminded herself with a deep sigh. "Christmas won't be the same!"

When the first day of Christmas arrived, the princess crawled from her bed. She descended the stairs one at a time, her night robes trailing behind her. Why hurry with so few presents to open? She ate Christmas breakfast quietly with her parents in the great hall.

The family moved to sit next to the warmth of the blazing stone fireplace. The castle servants appeared, bringing three beautiful presents wrapped in fabric and ribbons and other lovely trimmings.

Beautiful, the princess thought to herself. *But only three.*

"Would you like to open your gifts?" asked the king. The girl nodded. The family prayed, thanking God for the example of the wise men and for the True Gift of Christmas.

The princess hesitated, her heart a little heavy in her chest. She peeled away the wrapping of the first gift slowly and carefully. With only three gifts to open, she forced herself to take her time; otherwise, Christmas as she knew it would be over in no time at all.

fter a careful rolling back of the silken wrap, the first gift was revealed. Shiny with polish, a lovely wooden box carved with beautiful scrollwork seemed to smile at the princess, a gold latch on its face. Another gift within lay hidden in glittering fabric.

"A cake?" the girl questioned.

"The recipe calls for rare spices," explained her mother. "Smell."

The princess leaned over the box, breathing in a heavenly mixture of spices. Her mouth began to water.

"It tastes even better," grinned her father. "And when you taste it, remember your sweetness in our eyes."

Well, it's not what I would have asked for, thought the princess, *but it looks beautiful—and delicious.*

The cake, its beauty as great as its aroma, gleamed with all manner of iced swirls. The royal bakers had taken hours to artfully apply their creamiest frosting. The princess hugged her parents and thanked them.

he second present rested inside a tooled leather bag. The princess tugged on the drawstrings of the heavy sack and peeked inside. She gasped, her eyes wide with wonder.

"It's gold!" she gulped. Sure enough, inside the bag stood a golden rocking horse with a jeweled saddle. The horse's eyes, carved from sapphire stones, sparkled like stars in the firelight.

"Yes, it is gold," her father smiled, "and a costly gift. But I chose it to help you remember the passing golden days of childhood. You will not always be young, but memories of your childhood can never be lost."

"And these days have been a most amazing gift to us," added her mother.

A new understanding made the princess' heart beat fast. These were no ordinary gifts. Her parents' words touched her heart in a new and precious way.

"Thank you," she whispered as she kissed both parents gently.

"It is our delight," sighed the king. "And now for the last gift."

**I**nside a velvet bag with a gold cord sat the final gift. Out of this beautiful covering the princess lifted a gorgeous bottle of scented oil. As she viewed the liquid by the light of the fire, she saw that its contents shimmered—like diamonds.

"Ooooh," the princess murmured.

"Soon you will be a young lady," said her mother. "This special oil takes its fragrance from rare flowers, like you—our own unique flower."

"And yes, my dear, crushed diamonds float in the bottle too. But no diamond in the world could be more magnificent than you." The king smiled and his eyes became bright with tears.

The princess did not know what to say. She fell into her parents' arms.

"We love you, darling," said the queen as the family embraced.

Quiet stole over the great room now except for the crackle of logs on the fireplace. Only three gifts. But as the royal family held each other, each one felt a strange assurance. Somehow these gifts would be enough.

he princess carried the gifts to her room.
One by one, she lined them up on a shelf.

What would she do now? She could dab the oil on her wrists.
She could gaze at the beautiful horse and set it to rocking.
She could eat the cake.

But instead, she sank into a chair to ponder her parents' words.

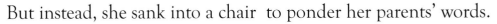

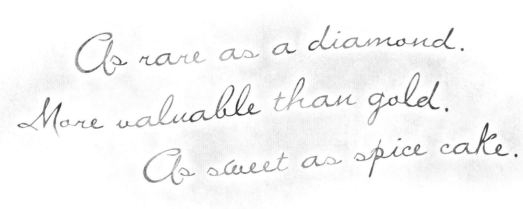

As rare as a diamond.
More valuable than gold.
As sweet as spice cake.

The princess sat quietly for some time,
thinking about her gifts and the meaning
of each one.

On the second day of Christmas, the many happy festivities included visiting relatives, entertainers and wonderful food and games. The princess was thoughtful, but looking forward to the holiday fun.

Unexpectedly, a heartbreaking tragedy interrupted the day's preparations. One of the castle stable hands fell from a lively horse and died that morning.

The family of this hardworking husband and father fell into deep sadness. Known by everyone at the castle, they had always served the royal family with joy. Now, at a time when they should be laughing and exchanging Christmas greetings, they received words of sympathy and tears. One daughter, the same age as the princess, could be comforted by no one.

 omething strange happened to the princess in the following days. She had hoped to enjoy her special cake at a time of her own choosing. She could imagine breaking off tender morsels and tasting them, one by one. But now, as she watched the palace cooks preparing food for a funeral meal, she did not feel hungry.

After speaking with her father, the princess and he hurried to the cottage of the stable hand's family. The princess carried a carved box. Once inside, she went to the grieving girl who bowed immediately in the presence of the royal family. The girl's mother looked on in bewilderment and fell to her knees.

"This special cake is filled with rare spices," said the princess. Then she knelt with the girl and her mother. "When you taste it, you will recall sweet memories of your dear father who lives in heaven now."

As she handed the cake to the young girl, everyone shed tears of both sorrow and joy. The daughter kissed the princess' hand and a smile slowly appeared on her wet, troubled face. Surprised, the princess felt happier than if she had kept the cake for herself.

Back at the castle the queen hugged the princess. "Your sweetness has grown with your sacrifice," she said.

 few days later a beggar came to the castle stairs. "Alms! Alms!" he cried. The princess watched the man limp in his layers of rags back and forth across the snowy castle stairs. Her heart broke as she thought of his poor cold feet and his empty stomach. Finally, unable to look any longer, she ran to her father.

"Father," she whispered. "Is my golden horse worth enough to buy a place for the beggar man to stay? Or some food? Or some clothes, or wood for a fire?"

"You would give your Christmas gift away for this man?" the king asked, wide-eyed.

"If it would not make me seem ungrateful to you, Father," she replied, nodding slowly.

ff they went to a landowner who had a cottage for sale. The princess bought the common, cozy house along with enough wood for the winter and enough food to last until spring.

Excited by this new adventure, the princess could scarcely breathe. The old man, seeing his new home for the first time, burst into tears and thanked the generous girl.

"Highness, nobody ever showed me any kindness afore today," he cried. "Bless ye, bless ye, oh, bless ye!"

The princess' heart hammered, and her own eyes filled with tears. "Welcome to your new home," she said, sniffling and helping the man up. "Be warm and filled, and happy Christmas to you!"

As the man rejoiced over his new surroundings, the princess wept openly in her father's arms. The king's heart filled with joy and pride. What a change he saw in his daughter!

 violent blizzard began during the next week and all sought shelter from the blinding snow. Late on the twelfth night of Christmas, the king and queen heard a knock at their door.

"Forgive me, Your Majesties," said the housemaid, shouting from outside, "but we desperately need your help. Someone dear to you is in danger!"

"Our daughter?" the queen cried, springing up.

"No, no," said the servant. "The princess lies safe in bed. 'Tis another who needs you!"

The king came to the door where his servant explained the events at hand and took orders to bring help immediately. Dressing himself hastily after a few words to his wife, he raced from the room. The queen also put on warm clothes and followed him a few minutes later, calling for servants to help.

Neither the king nor the queen noticed the pair of quiet feet following a short distance behind, or the young voice asking her own questions of the servants.

"She cannot be moved," a midwife reported when the king and queen reached the stable. "We brought her to shelter from the carriage in the snowdrift outside. But she can go no further."

n the hay, next to the horses, lay a woman familiar to both the king and queen. The king embraced the woman's worried husband, a dear friend from a southern kingdom, and took him aside. The queen climbed quickly into the hay next to her friend.

"What are you doing here, sister of my heart?" she asked, kissing the woman on both cheeks and embracing her.

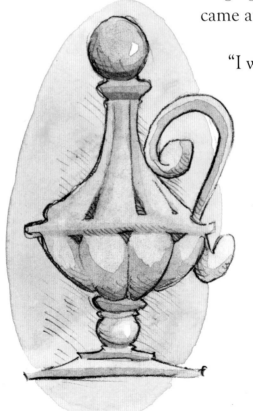

"Bringing a Christmas surprise," she whispered. "We thought we had time, but the storm came and... " With this, she cried out in pain.

"I will not leave you," said the queen, taking her hand.

Very soon, with the help of the midwife, the woman lay calm again and a new sound rang out—the cry of a baby boy.

At that moment, the king and the baby's father appeared with the little princess, who carried her bottle of oil.

**n**o one asked why, as the princess held out the bottle to the baby's mother. As in days of old, Christmas had come in its fullness. A baby had been born. A gift had been given.

"Are you certain?" the queen questioned, a tear in her eye.

"Yes, Mama," said the girl, smiling. "Giving makes the best Christmas of all."

"Christmas is here," whispered the king.

The baby fell into a sound sleep. And angels, silent to human ears, sang in the stars for joy.

"It is more blessed to give than to receive." Acts 20:35 (NIV)